www.ingramcontent.com/pod-product-compliance
Lightning Source LLC
Chambersburg PA
CBHW070636130626
46555CB00006B/2565

* 9 7 8 1 9 5 0 4 3 9 9 4 2 *

ACKNOWLEDGMENTS

This printed version of Rats and Bolts was created as a thank you to my Patreon community. I'm always looking for things to give them, because they give me so much. We're working towards something big. (Join us)

HONORARY CREW OF THE ATALAN
Your support keeps the ship in good health and spirits
Bella Darkwood
Alledria Hurt
Carmen Loup

ELITE ZOMBIE TAGGERS
A special thank-you to Zombie Tagger,
Austen Rodgers, for encouraging me to live my dream
Barbara Casaceli, for your sweet comments
JJ Falco, for reading everything I write
Richard Casaceli, for your continued support
Rheanna Summers, for your livestream dedication
Weatherly Camacho, for being an excellent homie

SPACE CAPTAINS OF SPACE
A super special thank-you to Space Captain,
Stephen Hamrick, for the opportunities I've been given

To those looking for their space family

ONE

The salvage title courier ship was Frankie's first 'adult' purchase, and as such, it hadn't been a very good one. Also, it wasn't a purchase. It was a lease. Xavier-class ships were minnows in the expanse of outer space, with hulls only as durable as their energy shields. What it lacked in size, power, and safety features, it made up for in crew quarters. Individual sleeping quarters with narrow beds, built-in shelving, and enough room to turn in a circle – at least for moderately sized species.

Nurflans were a moderately sized species, although Frankie was definitely on the smaller end of the species' range. The species was humanoid in shape – Frankie imagined an elder Nurflan would shake their head at Frankie's perspective, lecturing that 'a Nurflan should think that humans looked Nurflanian.' But Frankie had been adopted into an Earth family, and had always considered her soft scaled body the outlier rather than the norm.

On Nurfla, the patina of her scales would declare her generational family, and would communicate her emotions as part of full, nuanced conversation. On Earth, humans were often offended by the broadcast expressions. It seemed emotions were meant to be hidden, only to be disclosed in precise amounts after a certain number of dinner dates. This, and other contentions, only furthered Frankie's overwhelming desire to strike out on her own.

She leased a ship, hired a crew, and set off, all on a shoe-string budget. Which meant accepting low paying transport jobs just to reach the next planet and port – where surely, they'd find better luck.

"Captain, we're approaching the cargo's final destination," remarked Lorav over her furred shoulder. As pilot, Lorav often described their position in space and its relevancy to their assignment. It was accurate, although not always helpful.

Beside Lorav was her sister, Patav. Patav was a weapons specialist. When Frankie had hired the pair of Rapcorhs, they had immediately unbolted the pilot's console and moved it over beside the weapons console, close enough that they could sit shoulder-to-shoulder. As captain, Frankie hadn't approved of the remodel. Not only was it probably a violation of her lease agreement, it also blocked her view of the ship's windscreen that

relayed pertinent information. But Frankie permitted it; there was really no separating the two specialists. Well, except for the doctor who had. Rapcorhs were born in groups, often connected. When a set of Rapcorhian siblings reached maturity, they made a decision to remain physically connected or not. Lorav and Patav had decided to separate, but not by much. The sisters looked similar, but not identical like some human multiple births. They both had broad shoulders, square features, flat smoky coats, and one antenna off to the side, as if typically there were two.

Even looking around the stocky sisters at their consoles, Frankie couldn't miss the much larger ship which filled up a significant portion of the windscreen as they drew closer to the planet.

"Is that supposed to be here?"

"Uh, I don't think so. It's a ship-shipping ship and this planet isn't equipped to accept Class RHH cargo," said Patav.

Frankie tried to remember the acronym, but could only recall her own mnemonic – 'Really Honkin' Heavy'. So, it couldn't have business at the planet Raeth's Transportation and Distribution Center. The post office – as the center was often called in verbal hurries – didn't service anything that large.

"It's moving to intercept," said Lorav, who occasionally reported on the position of other ships in space, and the position's relevancy to the courier ship's chances of survival.

"Rail guns charging," said Patav, which is something a weapons specialist would say. Of some concern though, was the fact that Xavier-class ships like the one they sat in, didn't have rail guns.

"Compi, send a message on the cargo ship's frequency," Frankie asked of the ship's computer software.

What would you like the message to say?

"This is Farkhanix —" Frankie disliked her birth name, but the assumptions that others made when they heard it gave her an advantage in these situations. "— of the *Atalanta Empress*, registered as Franklin and Sons' Couriers. We see you're preparing your weapons. Is it for us? Or, maybe we're just in the way? I'm asking for a friend. I mean, me. I'm asking for me."

Unsurprisingly, she received no answer.

"Maybe the post office hired the ship for protection," suggested Lorav.

That would be unusual. The airspace above the post office was usually a peaceful one, except for maybe small traffic jams, road rage, and a queue that could go on for

4

weeks – also the Anaphylactic Bubble Wrap Incident of 2076. Still, it was worth a shot.

Frankie tried the planet's traffic control. "This is Farkhanix of the *Atalanta Empress*. There seems to be a hostile ship obstructing our landing. Do you know anything about it?"

Lorav maneuvered the Xavier-class ship to land on the planet, while trying not to provoke the gunners manning the other ship's Xavier-class-ship-sized weapons.

Flight, please be aware of—

The crew didn't catch the end of the sentence from traffic control as their small ship shook with a small fury.

"Oh, mevix," cursed Frankie. Her pink skin pulsed a bright coral in anger. "Fire back, I guess."

Patav and Lorav communicated with each other in a mixture of their home language and their triplet-speak to coordinate movement and weapons fire, disabling one of the bigger ship's many rail guns. Frankie had no idea what they had done to offend the large whale of a ship. They were both couriers of a sort, and not the sort in competition with each other. Their ship transported ships, biodomes, and satellites. Her Xavier-class ship delivered like... stellar panels and tea towels.

They took another hit.

"Damage report?" asked Frankie to the person on her right, who'd been uncharacteristically quiet during the

larger ship's appearance and attack, as if waiting for a personal introduction.

As second-in-command, Tarke was stationed to Frankie's right – although lounged was a more apt description. When Frankie had first met Tarke in primary school, she hadn't seen any likeness to a lioness as the humans had teased. Instead, she just saw someone who was different, like her. But while Frankie felt like an outsider, Tarke used her uniqueness to climb to the top of the popularity ladder. She'd pulled Frankie along with her clique, demanding she stop apologizing for her colors, and helped her come out of her shell. Not literally, though. Frankie wasn't cortaneous; she had no shell from which to emerge.

"You can look at it just as well as I can," retorted Tarke, her eyes flitting back and forth on her screen. They had become the best of friends, and just as quickly, gotten on each other's nerves. Still, Tarke was the first crew member Frankie had hired when she got the ship. The ship whose damage report Frankie couldn't see, because Lorav's square head was directly in the way.

Frankie challenged this retort by looking around Tarke's meaty leg, which was coated in a fine layer of fur and strategically propped onto her command console. Turned out, Tarke couldn't see the damage report either,

because some Earth reality TV show was playing on her screen.

"Can you do that in your free time?" asked Frankie.

"This is my free time. I don't have anything to do until you keel over." She ruffled her long mane – today it was teased into a shaggy poof, like the singers in Tarke's favorite retro-metal rock bands – as if perhaps it was just her duty to look pretty and wait.

"How about you give me the mevix damage report?" she shot back at Tarke.

"We're skagforged," she said simply after glancing over its contents.

Skagforged was an unprofessional phrase for 'screwed'. Then, Tarke promptly brought her show back up, not bothering to hide it anymore. On screen, humans in matching uniforms and utility belts chased a man without pants in between domiciles.

"See, this guy—" Tarke started to explain.

"Ground Control, we are taking fire. Please advise," broadcast Frankie, using a professional phrase for 'What the Skagforg?'

Sorry, we can't take any defensive measures. We've got better things to do, Flight.

"Better things to do than their job?" asked Frankie, staring down Tarke through her dark goggles.

Tarke shrugged and batted her eyes underneath long black lashes. Her flat nose flared ever so slightly.

Frankie's stomach turned as Lorav barrel-rolled and Patav rapidly fired, causing the tiniest inertial kickback but still adding another axis to their motion. Their verbal communication had ended and the sisters worked as one, leaving Frankie to guess which way she'd be jerked next.

So, it was a surprise when the ship started nose diving toward the post office at a speed which would not be sustainable once they met the ground.

Her second-in-command, ground control, and pilot didn't seem invested in keeping them alive and well. Should she take the day off too? Sneak in a few Earth cat videos before they were shot out of the sky or help to steer the ship into something massive and unmoving?

If it was a game of chicken her crew were playing, Frankie lost as she shrieked, "Am I the only one trying to come out of this alive?!"

Lorav didn't respond or change directions immediately, but Patav began firing energy pulses into the ground. Patav's handiwork created a trench with just enough room for Lorav to pull up and run parallel to imminent destruction. Even with the trench, Frankie could feel their tail end kicking up dirt. A warning that landing gear had not been deployed flashed on the big screen. Forget the runway, the Atalan settled at the post

office's front door, taking out a parking meter in the process.

"Here we are," said Lorav brightly, her toothy smile nearly wrapping around her square nose. Her eyes shined with pride.

Frankie peeled her fingers off the arm rests. Maybe having part of the windscreen blocked was a good thing.

"You scared the captain," said her sister, who didn't need her empathic skills to come to that conclusion. Frankie's skin had turned from bright coral to a muted, greenish-pink.

The ship above them stopped firing, Frankie assumed out of fear of hitting the post office they had parked so close to. Deciding not to cause an inter-corporate incident, the ship took off with as few words as they'd spared during their attack.

Frankie pressed the ship's intercom. "Brian, damage report?"

Brian replied, his voice groggy, as if he was waking from a nap. Frankie hoped that wasn't the case. *We've arrived.*

That wasn't a damage report.

"Anything need to be repaired for next takeoff?"

Nah, you should be good.

Frankie flicked her personal tablet to a map of the ship and saw his signal coming from his chambers. As the post

office-sanctioned mechanic and liaison, Brian did more liaising than anything else. And he didn't do much of that.

Wow, that was a bumpy ride, came the voice of their cargo supervisor through the intercom. *It was like a pinball game back here.*

Lorav and Patav exchanged confused glances. Frankie didn't bother to explain. It was always more trouble than it was worth, especially since half the time she knew the meaning of the idiom, but not its origin.

"Sorry about that, Gail. How's the cargo down there?"

The cargo? What about me? I'm an old lady. I could have broken a hip.

That seemed unlikely. To counter the issues an eighty-year-old widow from Earth might have, Gail had preemptively replaced many of her failing body parts with bionic devices. Besides replacing her pelvis and reinforcing her back with a titanium alloy, she'd also opted to replace her arms, which were withering with osteoporosis. The technology had opened up her post-retirement options and she now worked as Cargo Supervisor and Transporter of Really Heavy Things.

"Prepare the shipment for delivery," said Tarke.

It was prepared until we crash landed! I've now got to sort it all out again.

"I think the determination of 'crash' should take into account that we were being shot at. This landing was

more of an evasive maneuver than anything else," defended Lorav over the speaker.

Well, I don't blame the shooters one bit. I'd like to shoot you myself. If you guys keep mistreating me, I'll find one of those senior citizen cruise ships, drink mai tais on the deck in my hover chair, and visit the top ten planets with a knitting theme as judged by SpaceSeniors.com. Then the only thing I'd have to sort is birthday cards for my grandkids.

"Should we notify your grandkids that you've crash landed?" asked Lorav.

Uh, no, I don't think that will be necessary.

As far as Gail's family knew, she was already on one of those cruises. Gail kept up the charade by sending them postcards whenever their work landed them on a SpaceSeniors.com destination planet. She had even gone as far as doing video chats with cruise deck and beach backdrops, sipping a mai tai. That part was true. She liked mai tais, and she did drink a lot of them.

"We'll be down to help you out," apologized Frankie, feeling bad that she hadn't announced to batten down the hatches. The postal official would be out with her paperwork any moment to meet with Brian. In fact, they were usually out by the time the ship landed. Probably didn't want to catch crossfire or an earful.

TWO

They marched down to the cargo bay, where Gail was a fury of mechanical arms and boxes. Frankie bobbed back and forth, trying to enter the sorting fray like an industrial game of double-dutch rope. Eventually, she gave up and just listened to Gail gripe.

Tarke opened the bay's doors and mimed kissing the parking lot ground.

Lorav said, "You're welcome," while Patav ignored the gesture.

Frankie had seen it before, Lorav responding to the thoughts. Patav responding to the emotions.

Gail brought out the stacked boxes – knowing just how much clearance she'd need. It had to be at least two galactic tons of cargo. Frankie couldn't recall what was in them. She focused on flying the ship. And actually, Lorav did that, so maybe she just sat around like Tarke.

But the Atalan, formally the *Atalanta Empress*, was hers, or at least would be hers in sixty more EZ lease-to-

own payments – and she was proud of it. They had become the best couriers in this sector, with deliveries that arrived quickly and with minimal piracy loss.

Still no one had emerged to accept the goods. Nor did Brian waltz by them to execute one of his few responsibilities.

"Don't bother setting them down, Gail, I'll just be a moment," she said as she passed the woman. She would go in Brian's stead. She had a few choice words to share anyway.

"Sure, as if they aren't heavy," Gail replied sourly.

For Gail, they weren't, but she made faces all the same.

The entrance revealed a narrow hallway which solely led to a clerk's window. Along the walls, motion-activated advertisements and notices created a flashy tunnel full of lost and found dog pods knocked off course, fertisrat exterminators, missing persons, and the Galaxy's Most Wanted. A pink- and purple-hued Nurflan with massive cannons strapped to her back cocked her hip and winked, posing for her wanted poster. The woman resembled Frankie, same species, same color family. However, the fugitive did not wear radiation goggles, or much else. One million credits.

Frankie hadn't managed to pull her eyes off the poster as she rang the bell on the clerk's sill.

"Please don't do that." A generic bald white head rose into view. Frankie could tell he didn't mean 'please'.

"Then why is it there?" asked Frankie. "I figured no one knew we were here since the office didn't come to our aid. Why are you letting pirates circle overhead?"

"We will send someone out there shortly to retrieve the shipment. Any damage to the shipment to report?" The pale head bobbed.

"No, no thanks to you. If you cared about the shipment, you should have protected our ship."

"What's the order number?" he asked, continuing to ignore her.

Frankie got on her radio. "Gail, what's the order number?"

"You mean to say, you went in there and didn't even have the order number? What about your papers? Do you even know what you're delivering?"

"Dolphin-safe tuna?" guessed Frankie.

"No, that was last week. We're delivering sixty tons of fuel in packages compatible with the Norma 6B-style vending machines."

"Manfloon's Appendix, if the ship had taken more damage, we might have exploded. You really need to tell us when we're shipping hazardous cargo."

"I did tell you. I tell you every morning in the briefs I send out. Did you read the brief this morning?"

Frankie didn't read the briefs if she could help it. Where was Brian? This was his job.

Gail didn't stop there. "And you really need to tell me when we're taking fire, so that I can secure the cargo, so we don't explode."

Fair enough.

"So, uh, what's the order number?"

Gail pushed the talk button on her radio just to sigh into it.

"Received," said the peg head clerk, watching his screen. A stiff hand came from behind the window and rang the bell on the sill.

Warmth crept up Frankie's neck and face – warmth she knew was accompanied by another shade of pink.

"That's how it feels," he said before his head lowered from view.

The fugitive on the wanted poster mimed laughter as Frankie sulked out of the building.

With Gail's help, the shipment was loaded into ugly neon orange trucks. Fluorescent coloring communicated sexual arousal in Frankie's species, pervading much of the Nurflan advertising. Sexy doughnuts. Sexy vehicles. Sexy cereal. Neon sells. The trucks looked like obscene promotions for the transportation of goods.

A voice behind Frankie startled her. "It seems the order is accounted for."

Two hefty green beings with clipboards pressed close to her. They had the consistency of dense Jell-O, but their viscous bodies slimed more than jiggled. One wore an Astros baseball hat.

"You're welcome." Tarke said as she sidled up to Frankie. She was a head taller than Frankie, but her hair made her that much more so. Tarke brushed it up with her hand, fighting the gravity of the planet. She had a habit of tweaking the ship's gravi-stat to accentuate the day's hairstyle. She said the lower gravity levels also fought aging, but that it was too late for Gail.

"No one has explained to us why there were pirates overhead," tried Frankie again. If this was going to be a common occurrence, they needed to know. Lorav and Gail waited for the explanation as well, hands on hips.

"It's just a pissy courier ship," dismissed the one sans hat.

"Biting the hand that feeds it…" said Gail.

"We don't feed it anymore, but yeah, still bad form. We also don't feed you either. I am pleased to inform you that the quantum-dimensional transport system, trademarked Instant Teleport! is now fully operational. As such, all deliveries will now be made through the quantum realm. Your services are no longer needed,"

recited the one with the baseball hat, idly referring to his clipboard held by a protrusion of his slime.

"Uh, what?" asked Frankie. That transport system touted instantaneous delivery by porting items into and out of the quantum realm, but it was donkey's years away from functionality. The ending position of the object was difficult to direct with any amount of precision, and often objects reformed in and around other objects and people.

"There was a breakthrough in the technology. The cargo no longer arrives scrambled, and it also arrives at its intended location about eighty percent of the time."

"But that's awful statistics."

"It's no worse than the statistics for the couriers."

"Not *our* statistics!" Frankie turned bright coral.

"Well, we can't keep the postal system up just for you, now can we? Besides you're infinitely slower than Instant Teleport!™."

At that moment, Brian walked by with a rolling book bag.

"Where are you going?" asked Frankie. She had a bone to pick with him.

"I come with your contract. No contract, no mechanic."

Mevix.

"Can you at least finish the diagnostics so we're not stranded?" Frankie tried as yellow pigmented her skin.

"Sure." Brian looked at the paneling on either side of the ship's cargo bay. "Looks safe enough."

With a bro-boy chin lift, he walked into the post office.

"He already knew. That's why he's been hiding out," concluded Lorav.

Frankie hadn't noticed any change in his cooperation.

"Did you catch whether he bothered to do any safety checks after our—" Frankie realized to whom she was talking, "—impressive landing?"

"I wouldn't count on it." A hiss and a sharp clanking noise escaped the engine room, startling them all. "I'm not even sure he was a mechanic."

Mevix.

A tiny grouping of ankle-high rodents ran by. One stopped to sniff the cargo bay ramp. Gail tried to smash it with her foot but it scurried away.

"What is that?" asked Frankie, slightly horrified.

"Fertisrats… that pissy ship dropped them off here," the slime answered. He turned to his partner. "This entire department is being let go with the conclusion of this delivery. Your services are no longer needed. You have been laid off."

In return, his partner laid him off as the final act of whatever their job was. They tossed their clipboards behind their shoulders. A fertisrat carried the objects off.

"Do you want to grab a beer?"

"Sure, I gotta assess my career options."

"Another clipboard job?"

"Totally."

The trucks departed with the green blobs.

"Did we at least get paid?" asked Tarke.

"Of course," said Gail. "I hold the packages until we receive payment. We received 42 GRL and 100 credits."

"Credits?" Galaxy Regulated Loot was the only currency backed by the Galactic Treasury & Health Department. It was mostly used for government jobs.

"Toward shipping through Instant Teleport!™."

"That's it?! What about severance?" demanded Tarke.

"No severance for contract workers, unless you steal some fuel cells," said Frankie, thinking of the long-gone courier ship turned pirate. "We should have split them with that ship-shipping ship. That's why they were firing at us."

"You couldn't have known," said Lorav and Patav in unison.

While she agreed that she couldn't read the minds of their silent cohort, she refused to let herself off the hook concerning this layoff. She should have had her finger on the pulse. She'd just assumed that the technology would need to be perfect, but obviously it just had to be better than her. Now they were out of a job. And after two or

three EZ missed payments, they'd also be homeless. Frankie turned a melon color. She was going to be sick.

They all climbed back into the ship, a little defeated, a little tired, and super pissed off.

"Well, I know what I'm doing with my 8.20 GRL. Drinks!" Tarke shouted in the direction of the post office as the cargo bay doors closed.

"Shouldn't we invest the GRL into our next venture?" asked Gail.

The thin eyebrows seemed to float on her fur as Tarke raised them. "I just lost my job and you want to take my money? Why don't we use some of your retirement fund?" She looked to Frankie for support, but was clearly angry with both of them.

Frankie felt herself flash fuchsia. "I don't know, Tarke. You might have to take one for the team. I just don't think distributing this last payment is in the crew's best interest."

"Take one for the team? Best interest? Yeah, you know what would have been in our 'best interest'?? You pulling your head out of the Atomic Number 14 to read the writing on the wall before all the horses ran off, and any other metaphors that mean you skagforged us." Tarke stormed through the cargo bay, toppling anything adjacent to her path that was not bolted down.

"I could fix her a Mai Tai," said Gail, taken aback.

"I don't think it's about the drinks. I'll go talk to her," replied Frankie. She imagined it wouldn't be the only uncomfortable conversation she'd have today.

Frankie climbed the stairs to the upper level of the ship. The censor beeps and yelling of a reality TV show echoed through the corridor line with round brass submarine doors on either side. Frankie knocked on the one with all the glam band stickers on it.

The television volume increased and Frankie didn't know if she had been heard or not. It didn't much matter, as either scenario led to Frankie banging on the door firmly, continuously, and persistently.

Tarke gave in after only forty seconds with a squawk of consent. Frankie opened the round door and settled her weight into the nearly vertical tube. Avoiding the ladder on the opposite side, she slid down onto a pile of laundry. Tarke had at first convinced Gail that laundry was part of her duties and Gail had dropped Tarke's clean laundry down the chute. That had been months ago and the pile still remained. At least it softened the fall. The entries had been designed to maximize the floor and wall space of the tiny shoe box. It also kept stuff from floating out of the room when gravity shifted.

Tarke lazed on her narrow bed stacked high with an assortment of blankets and pillows. Frankie had never

seen the bed made. Even when Tarke had moved in, she had only scooped up the bedding on her originating bed and thrown it onto the destination bed. Despite the evident enjoyment of nesting in soft things, Tarke had one leg raised and propped up against the wall, which, like all the other vertical space, was filled with posters and logo stickers of Tarke's favorite bands from all over the universe. Frankie recognized the polyphonic singers of Uutoh, The Radio Waves who refused to record anything and instead only broadcast out into the universe, and even the album art for some classical Gregorian chants, to name a few. She would have scolded Tarke for putting stickers on the walls of the leased ship, but at least they were contained to her quarters.

At the end of the bed, her television continued to blast. A ridiculous looking Earthling chased another, but neither looked like law enforcement. Apparently, a lot of Earth TV was running, which was silly because the humans really weren't that good at it.

"Just thought I'd catch up on my shows since we don't have jobs anymore. Did you know North America still has unemployment benefits? Who knew you could benefit from being unemployed? I mean besides having time to watch your shows. This guy, he tried to apply for those benefits, but he's wanted for a crime. The guy chasing him, Cat, also doesn't qualify for unemployment,

because he makes too much finding criminals like this guy and turning them in for rewards. Self-employment, I guess."

Earth was a weird place. Frankie did not regret leaving.

"We could do that you know," continued Tarke. "Turn in some warrants for money. It really doesn't look that hard."

The man was now riding on a small scooter through an airport. Everyone was laughing and jumping out of the way. Frankie thought of the posters in the post office.

"You mean like the Galaxy's Most Wanted?"

"Uh, well, we'd probably start on someone a little easier first. Maybe some corporate gigs." Tarke pulled out her tablet and swiped through some documents. "This woman is in the same stellar system we're in now."

Tarke showed her a photo of a sleek and elegant woman with long dark green hair being near crowded out of the frame by her own tentacles, a Kieron.

"What's the reward on her?" asked Frankie, curious.

"One thousand GRLs' equivalent (EGRL). And that's just Microlutions's reward. If that corporation wants them, then Vigar Industries, Pi Zeconis, etc. probably do too. When she's captured, we can negotiate a higher bounty," Tarke said matter-of-factly as if they were already in pursuit.

"Watching a bounty-hunting television show in the same stellar system as a wanted fugitive isn't exactly a qualification for something like this."

"I'm just saying, that while we flounder for another regular gig," submitted Tarke as Frankie flashed fuchsia again, "we can keep our eye out for unique opportunities. And you know, if we can write a reality show around it, then even better."

Frankie couldn't tell if she was joking or not.

"Speaking of which, you know I can't disburse this money. We need fuel. I'll pay you back when I can."

"So you messed up. That doesn't mean you can take my beer money."

Frankie might have changed colors, but more indicative was her nose making a sniffing, snorting sound.

Tarke opened her lean soft arms and pulled Tarke in to her chest and nest of bedding. Frankie curled up, whimpering about failing the crew.

Tarke cooed. "I'm with you. We're all with you. That courier job was boring anyway. I volunteer my beer money toward the fuel fund, but I think we're going to have to hit up one of those fuel cell vending machines."

The irony was not lost on Frankie and she managed a smile before snuggling closer to her friend.

THREE

Hey Captain, can I get your ear for a moment? Gail's voice pressed through the intercom.

Frankie's tears had dried by now, but her voice still cracked when she answered in the affirmative. Tarke hand-combed the hair and pressed a damp wash rag to her leader's face. Frankie said her thanks before climbing out of Tarke's bedroom. She had come to straighten out an unruly staff member, and instead was comforted by the woman who always had her back.

Frankie retraced her steps through the corridors to the cargo bay. In this expansive universe jobs came and went, as did the crews who performed them, but she had handpicked her crew, plucking them from their home worlds, promising adventure, protection, and buttloads of money. She saw them as family, and at the same time, Frankie was already stretched thin by the EZ payments and payroll.

The *Atalanta Empress* had a lot of junk in her trunk, or at least the capacity for it. The cargo bay was large enough to contain a couple terrain vehicles or 50 G-tons of fuel. She wished they had either. On one wall, clipboards much like the ones the slimes had were hanging along the wall, all contracts with the transportation system that had gone defunct.

A sigh came from behind a worktable. Gail was on all fours with her head lowered. "I'm actually kind of ashamed."

A coolness traveled along Frankie's skin as she racked her brain for embarrassing ailments that an old lady on the floor might have.

"Did you uh, have an accident?" she asked hesitantly.

"More of an oversight." Gail stood up and raised her bronze hand to reveal a screw she'd been chasing under the table. Dust left gray streaks in her short silver white hair. "The fuel cells we delivered are self-weighing, but looking over the ship log, I realized the cells weighed less than stated in the order and the manifest. I didn't realize until I went over the standing contract."

"The math's off? Has someone contacted us for an investigation?"

"No, I just—"

"Then, I don't really care." Frankie cut her off.

"I just wanted to bring it to your attention, Captain." She said, her voice subdued. With a modified spine and exoskeleton pants resolving the woman's osteoporosis, she easily stood a head over Frankie, but now she stooped as much as her augmentations would allow.

Frankie hadn't meant to lash out at the human. They seemed pretty sensitive to such things. Why did Gail think this was pertinent? Gail's time would be better spent sitting in front of that bounty-hunting TV show with Tarke.

Then, Frankie remembered the Kieron.

"Someone stole fuel?"

Gail lit up. "It's definitely an inventory loss, but I've never seen anything like it. I'd be surprised if Zimmer 1 or Raeth ever catches it. I barely did. And to pull it off on an intra-stellar system route…" Gail couldn't hide the admiration in her voice.

There was crime all over the galaxy, but an advanced technique in the same vicinity as a high-profile criminal might not be a coincidence.

"Tarke, please report to the cargo bay," Frankie broadcast.

A mumble and a groan echoed over the ship's intercoms. Frankie chose to believe it was acknowledgment, complaint, and 'on the way,' in three efficient syllables.

Tarke slunk more than walked. Shoulders, hips, and tail undulated as if the air she traveled through was more viscous than everyone else's. Behind her saunter, the triplets followed in single file. It was one of the few times the pair were stacked instead of parallel, only because the stairwell was narrow and the pair were broad.

"Oh dear, it's not that important," said Gail as her cheeks reddened to a russet with the arrival of more than Tarke.

Lorav and Patav had been recruited for Intergalactic Rugby League while they were still in secondary school, and they had played professionally for a while. Lorav had read plays and moves in her opponents' heads as if she were predicting the future. Patav on the other hand was distracted by all the rage, insecurities, fears, and attractions in the sport. She found she was filled with aggression all the time. The steroids they were both taking didn't help, either.

Since giving up that sort of profession, they had added a few pounds on the hips, which only made them look that much more intimidating. Frankie wondered if rugby had any transferable skills for overpowering fugitives.

"I sensed excitement," Patav explained their presence.

"Well, I don't know if it's anything," Frankie disclaimed her feeling.

"But, you have a good feeling," said Lorav.

Frankie gave her an odd look.

"You're thinking that you have a good feeling," clarified Lorav. "People don't think about their feelings often."

"If they did, maybe they'd make more rational decisions," said Frankie. Her kind used emotions as a communication device more than anything else. Having grown up on Earth, Frankie's emotions had taken on a different dynamic.

"I thought our feelings were always on our mind. We're emotional creatures," said Gail.

"No, that's the problem. You're constantly experiencing emotions and making decisions based on them, without ever wondering what the source of those emotions is."

"It's just how a lot of brains are wired," said Patav. "Even though I rationally know I'm sensing others' emotions, my brain still tries to ascribe my thoughts to them. We're thinkers driven by emotions."

"Yeah, yeah, thoughts, feelings, blah blah. Where's the action? Why'd you call me down here?" asked Tarke.

Gail gave Tarke the side eye. They had never really gotten along. She probably didn't want to field Tarke's questions and comments about an oversight.

Frankie started in the other direction first. "Tell us about the fugitive nearby."

"Are we hunting people?!" said Tarke more excitedly than she should have. When no one answered immediately, she pulled the memo back up on her tablet. "Kieron by the name of Quajalimk wanted by Microlutions INC for mechanical sabotage of one of their ships. This gorgeous gal was last seen in the Norma 6B system. You got an idea as to where she is?"

"Gail, tell them about the fuel cells."

"It was really a rather clever trick I've never seen done before. It could go into books about stealing things," Gail managed to share without providing context.

"So you think this fugitive was on the planet the fuel cells originated from?" asked Lorav.

Most people use 'so you think' to make sure they understand someone's point. The phrase took on an odd layered level with Lorav.

"Should we send a report to the authorities?" asked Patav.

"Mevix no!" said Tarke. "And let somebody else get the bounty? 1000 EGRL y'all. She doesn't even look tough. I bet even Gail could take her."

Both an insult and a joke since Gail's augmentations made her on par, if not stronger, than most of the rest of the crew.

"How do we know it's her?"

"You said she was a mechanic? It's her. This was a mechanical heist. I've never seen anything like that," repeated Gail.

"But, what did she do?" asked Patav. "Is she dangerous?"

Tarke fiddled with her tablet and brought up a news article.

"Skagforg," she said as she scrolled. "She sabotaged navigation and the autopilot. Microlutions partially foiled her attempt. She was aiming for a Pi Zeconis corporate building. Over 300 employees work there. They crash landed nearby."

"Casualties?" asked Frankie.

"No just one buttload of property damage, but mevix, if she had flown into that building…" She trailed off, not wanting to describe her next thoughts. Lorav didn't want to share them either.

"So, what is Pi Zeconis paying?" asked Lorav.

"Uh, nothing, it looks like. They say it's an Intergalactic Police matter or an internal matter for Microlutions."

"She can't expect to evade the authorities for long," commented Gail.

"Especially if we catch her first!" Tarke said, still scrolling through the article.

"Is this our only job lead?" asked Patav, the first to speak seriously on capturing the Kieron for financial gain.

Frankie wouldn't be entertaining this at all if they had another opportunity to earn revenue. "There are some delivery jobs floating around, but the bidding war is disgusting. We wouldn't even earn the fuel back," she said, dismayed.

"But our delivery rates are better than anyone and those stupid teleporters to boot."

"Supply over demand. There are millions of couriers. Our portfolio isn't going to matter."

"And those teleporters are pretty cool," admitted Gail.

"80% success rate?" asked Patav.

"You have to expect some amount of error when you're talking about billions of light years and billions of products. No one gets it completely right and they'll improve," said Tarke.

"Amazon gets it right," added Gail.

"Yeah, well, the Universe isn't run by Amazon," retorted Tarke.

"Yet," said Patav.

"Our best bet for courier business is in Barknik System, the opposite direction from Zimmer 1. We don't have enough fuel for both, so we have to pick," said Frankie.

"You're the captain. Don't you decide?" asked Tarke, hoping the decision would be in her favor.

"We've reached an end here. We all need to decide collectively what we'd like to do next. We could do this as a one-time gig, maybe earn some money to get everyone where they want to go, if it's not here with us."

"Or, we could try it out and love it!" said Tarke in a way that made the phrase sound much more like a threat than an objective possibility. "This is going to be so much fun. I love those shows…"

Lorav and Patav shook their heads at Tarke before nodding to Frankie. "We go where you go."

"Gail?" asked Frankie.

"I'm in. This woman is a pioneer in piracy. Thieves will make out like bandits, then the person who solves the issue will be able to sell it to the universe for an even larger payout."

"Why don't they open the shipments and count things?" asked Lorav.

"Millions of boxes and you want to *count the things*?"

"Well, not myself, particularly."

"Time is money. This technique, once it gets out, will cause a lot of problems," reported Gail.

"Captain?" asked Lorav.

"Don't thieves always make out like bandits?" wondered the captain out loud.

"No, not that."

"I don't have any better ideas, so I'm with you guys."

"We're with you."

"And I with you."

"Me too," said Gail.

Tarke ran through enough troubleshooting and safety checks to get the Atalan back in the air and then into outer space. Meanwhile, Lorav calculated and programmed the most fuel-efficient route to Zimmer 1. There was of course the "Optimize Fuel Efficiency" feature on their auto-navigation, but Lorav swore up and down that it calculated based on a mediocre manual pilot, which she was not. Tarke swore that if Lorav's strategies were programmed into the auto-navigation, it would be listed under "Optimize Tediousness."

As the ship used a lot of fuel traveling in subspace, Lorav had the ship jump in and out of the dimension and used planets to slingshot them while in typical space. It was a bumpy ride, but they'd have enough fuel left to make it to a second (close) destination without refueling.

Excitement hung in the air. Instead of slinking off to their rooms to let pilot and weapon specialist occupy the bridge, it was all hands on deck. Tarke convinced them to watch an episode of *Cat the Bounty Hunter* for research.

"You'll need to learn how criminals operate and also tricks for capture."

Cat was a thin and lanky fellow with a wiry graying hair. He wore a utility belt twice the size the police on Earth did, full of oddly shaped weapons. He pulled a long rifle from his back and aimed it at a loping quadruped. The outlaw's eyes narrowed in fear, homing in on his escape route. With a blast from the rifle, a net flew and wrapped around him.

He first tangled and tripped, but then he laughed. "Are you [BEEP]ing serious?" he asked.

It switched to a post-scene interview with Cat sitting at a McDonald's diner booth eating a corn-burger. "What I didn't realize at the time was that he was an ionic quadruped. It quickly turned into a skagforg."

Back to the chase, the outlaw glowed brightly within the fading net. When he finished absorbing its energy, he threw it off and launched into leaping bounds well over his previous range.

Cat grabbed a human child's hover board to follow. His large boots engulfed the surface of the board and then some. The human child shook its fist and shouted, but then busied itself scooping up the net and rifle. Other children ran out to fight over the found objects.

"Irresponsible, questionable ethics," muttered Gail, who must still have felt some attachment to Earth, even though Earth was primarily a movie studio now.

Cat finally caught up to the fugitive, who was slowing. He threw a cup of liquid frozen treat onto him and he shorted out, falling midleap.

"*Signs* wins again, mother[BEEP]," said Cat as he poked the prone being with a stick he previously had not been holding.

The quadruped sparked, but didn't move.

"Why does he keep beeping?" asked Lorav.

Frankie had questions too, like how much of this was scripted, but she decided not to offend her friend. Tarke's enthusiasm played a critical role in making sure no one thought too hard about what they were trying to accomplish.

"He's cursing," explained Gail.

"No, he said 'skagforg' earlier."

"It doesn't count."

Skagforg and mevix were universally the worst curses. Apparently, Earth thought otherwise.

Cat began to get suspicious and used his stick to turn over the fugitive, only to realize he was looking at the quadruped's decoy.

"[BEEEEEEEP]"

"Mevix, if that guy can't catch him, how do we think we're going to?" asked Lorav.

Frankie cringed. Had Lorav pulled that thought from her captain's head or had she just come to the same conclusion? Cat was supposedly a professional and forty-five minutes into the episode, he had no one in custody.

Tarke stood up behind her console like it was a podium, then addressed her crew members. "You see, his mistake is that he let the fugitive get out of his sight and it slipped into a cloning machine. You have to be aware of your surroundings."

Gail scribbled some notes on her tablet.

The show cut to Cat sitting on a stool at a different McDonald's, dipping corn-nuggets into corn sauce, recapping the previous scene.

"Man, I let the fugitive out of my sight and didn't realize we were so close to a cloning machine. In this job you have to be aware of your surroundings. Also…"

"You have to have the right weapons!" cut in Tarke.

"Using an electricity direction weapon against an electrical being was obviously another big mistake. I should have done my research. Remember—"

"Come prepared and leave with money!" said Cat and Tarke in unison. Tarke leaped up onto her console, fist in the air.

Even Gail giggled along with the others' hearty laughter.

Once Lorav could vacate her pilot's console for some time, they all went down to the cargo bay. The sisters threw Tarke around under the guise of training them on rugby moves that they might find useful. Gail took more notes. Frankie realized that none of the moves would be a match for a Kieron's agility and abundance of tentacles.

"Can we turn down the artificial gravity?" asked Tarke after being knocked down for the fortieth time. This time by a practicing Gail.

"No, then you won't understand the strength that will be required," replied Patav with a broad smile.

"At least let's put down mats" she argued as she rubbed her butt cheek and looked at Frankie for support.

"Does Cat use mats?" Frankie teased.

Eventually, Tarke identified a signature move of a particularly tanned wrestler on Earth and put an end to the sisters' education. And they soon were given a rundown of useful wrestling moves by Tarke, with everyone taking turns as the target.

Even if they didn't catch the fugitive, Frankie wouldn't regret this last round of merriment and glee.

FOUR

Ten hours after Frankie fell asleep, the lights in her room gradually brightened until she awoke. Any amount of space travel made circadian rhythms resemble a chaotic improvisation more than a well-measured chord progression, and each dealt with it in their own way. Gail, having spent a long life on Earth, struggled the most. She used a twelve-hour metronome to make sense of time passed as days and nights. Frankie set her 'night' as ten hours after she began to snore, letting her schedule shift naturally, losing only a few hours of sleep when planet business hours needed to be observed.

Frankie enjoyed her allotted time in the shower, letting her thin scales hydrate then air drying in the warmness of her small room. Her body took on a pink glow of contentment, which seemed to comfort her all the more. They had had a good night, and there was the opportunity for many more to come. While she waited for her kettle to heat up, she dressed in her scale-tight suit, covering up

all but her face and hands and the glow within faded. A group of clothiers once created a line of suits that projected light onto the user's face to mute the changing colors. They claimed it was perfect for inter-species business negotiations and poker games. They received a lot of backlash. Most traditional Nurflans viewed repressing the color to be the same as silencing a species. Frankie was torn. Humans found a great sense of shame with many of their natural emotions, and felt shame for her when her emotions were laid out for all to see. They saw her as a squishy thing who had lost her armor. While she understood Nurflan hesitancy on muting their colors, she also just thought it would make everyone else more comfortable if she weren't such an open book. Maybe she had appropriated some of the humans' shame.

The long-sleeved and long-legged suit was a compromise and Frankie wore it as she sat cross-legged in the captain's chair. Silence whirred around her, a reward for being the only one on deck. She removed her radiation glasses. Without Lorav's head in the way and her radiation glasses off, the screen glared too brightly.

"Compi, increase windscreen opacity by 40%."

When the screen dimmed, Frankie could distinguish the ship's movements in and out of subspace as they skipped and hopped to their destination. The brief stints

of subspace flickered in between scenes of the same stellar system, like a film.

The steaming mug she held turned her fingers an orange-red that glimmered like embers in a fire. Caffex, a drink consisting of heated crystals added to a water and citric acid mixture, was one of the few things she had adopted from her planet. It turns out any planet with technology advances had a perk-me-up drink. Humans used coffee and tea. Nurflans used crystals that emitted energy upon heating. Populations without an energy beverage slept in and were pretty chill, but also struggled to develop progressive technologies.

As her pilot slept, the ship followed her previously set course and implemented the collision prevention system to navigate around smaller obstacles, such as rogue asteroids (universally measured in multiples of Texas since the movie had made its rounds within the galaxies), other ships, and sometimes just a dense cloud of space dust. The auto correct could be rather aggressive. With the visual cues, Frankie began to feel the small jolts of inertia. Was her brain just filling in the blanks or was something off? Frankie ignored it until she couldn't.

"Compi, status report: inertial dampeners."

Inertial dampeners are working at 94%

That wasn't bad. It wasn't fantastic either. Frankie wished she had a mechanic to fix a couple things around here.

"What's the source of the inefficiency?"

Mechanic needed.

Frankie wasn't sure if that meant a mechanic was needed to identify the inefficiency, or if a missing mechanic was the inefficiency at this point.

"Report ship damages."

The computer began rattling off vital and inane systems in no particular order with varying degrees of damage. It seemed it was going to name every damaged beam in their clunker of a ship. A ship computer should allow the ship to run itself. She shouldn't need to hire a mechanic, but Compi apparently couldn't even differentiate critical versus benign damage in its report.

"Compi, tell me damage only pertinent to staying in the sky."

Atmospheric navigation is currently online.

"Forg it. I give up," she muttered.

Florida is the meth capital of the Milky Way, home to Florida Man and the Iteration Movie Studio. Florida—

She needed to upgrade Compi, and she needed a mechanic.

"Stop."

We are entering orbit over Zimmer 1. Would you like to abort the procedure?

"Maybe, I mean, no," breathed Frankie as a Vigar Industries ship in its periwinkle blue filled her screen.

The VI ship got its oblong shape from being built around a massive rail gun core. The ship itself was able to absorb a lot of the weapon recoil, making it efficient in warfare and solidifying VI's spot as one of the Big Players in the galactic commercial wars.

"All crew to the bridge. We've arrived and have already found trouble." *With a capital T*, she thought.

RING RING

"Let it through."

"Identify yourself," came the disconnected voice.

"Franklin and Sons' Courier Service, here to pick up some fuel for transport."

"Courier services are no longer needed for this Fuel Center. They are using Vigar Industries' new Instant Transport!™ teleportation system for the instantaneous shipment of goods."

"You don't say," said Frankie.

"Since there is no business here for you, kindly remove yourself from our airspace."

"It's a free galaxy. I can be here. Why don't you kindly remove yourself?"

"Please leave immediately."

"OK, we'll work on that," dismissed Frankie as she hung up on them. Well, as well as one could hang up on someone over radio frequencies.

"Well, I don't think I handled that well," admitted Frankie.

"I don't know. I'm kind of a fan of the 'I know you are but what am I?' retort," said Tarke, shuffling onto the bridge with pink bunny slippers, bed hair frizzing in several directions.

Frankie wasn't reassured by the statement. She had recently pulled Tarke's privilege of unsupervised business communications after a particularly nasty incident in which she had challenged the President of Panex to a Gregorian chant battle.

"You think they're here for the fugitive?" asked Lorav. The sisters and Gail had been slightly delayed in arriving, having taken the time to dress.

"I'm guessing that's a good bet," whispered Frankie.

"Yay!" shouted Gail, jumping with glee. Her braced feet clanged on the bridge floor.

"Yay? It's going to be much more difficult to get her if Vigar Industries is already here," said Patav.

"I'm just excited that we were right." Gail grinned.

"Do you think they know that we know?" asked Lorav.

"I bet they can figure it out. The promise of a thousand credits and a courier ship freshly laid off?" said Tarke. "We're not exactly an enigma."

"No, we're an Xavier model," explained Gail.

"Will you take us in for a landing?" Frankie asked Lorav.

"Probably. Let me uh, do a pre-landing check."

Unsurprisingly, none of her crew had checked on the landing gear after they landed without it earlier. Frankie gave her a look.

"Hey, it's the mechanic's job."

"And now it's yours."

"Why don't you make Tarke do it? She hardly does anything around here."

"Do you really want Tarke in charge of safe landings?"

Tarke had once called Brian in the middle of the night once to change a light bulb. Brian came thinking it was a booty-call. Turns out, she was just using the wrong light switch.

Lorav didn't answer, but instead settled into her seat and dutifully turned to her work console.

RING RING

"Ugh, go ahead and answer it," Frankie told the computer, slumping into her chair. Her Caffex had gone cold.

"We see you are preparing to land," the disconnected voice accused.

"Uh, yes, we plan to 'please leave immediately,' but our navigation system has gone wonky. We need to land to do a few repairs," Frankie tried.

"Negative. Please travel to the next-closest planet."

"Didn't I just tell you that our navigation system is a bust? We tried to go somewhere else, but we can't navigate there."

"Then manually drive your ass away from here. We are in the middle of important business."

"I'm sorry. We'll try to stay out of your way," Frankie reported. Then, to Lorav, "Put her down."

Patav hurried to her seat. There was a good chance that weapons would be a critical part of their landing, again.

The ring in the center of the VI ship glowed a more fluorescent periwinkle blue as they charged their rail gun, aiming toward the Atalan. Four minute white-silver ships emerged from the large ship with more maneuverability and less blast-you-into-the-next-galaxy weapons fare. The one closest planet-side let off a warning shot, which grazed Atalan's shields.

Shields at 30%.

"Yikes, put her down," responded Frankie.

"OK, hang on," said Lorav as she pressed on the joystick with particular angled force, avoiding a not-so-warning shot and pointing the ship's nose toward Zimmer 1.

Orbit is decaying too rapidly announced Compi helpfully.

"Fire at the mother ship if you can," commanded Frankie. The fighters were too agile for the courier ship, and they had no chance in Planet Hell to disable the mother ship, but perhaps they could distract them, shiny sparks and such.

Patav fired lasers, which decayed in the ship's force field, causing soft pink ripples, not unlike the blotches churning on Frankie's skin. With luck or because the sisters were master tacticians, one of the fighters flew into the laser's path without its shields up. The laser sliced part way into its hull.

The ship would automatically seal the damaged area and deploy mech-bots to fix the abrasion. Frankie wished her ship had a few mech-bots. Having 30% of all free GRL apparently had its perks. The small paper cut diverted attention for just moments, and that allowed Lorav to deftly maneuver to a loading area not far from the fuel depot. The ship convulsed and rattled, making everyone cringe.

"Were we hit?" asked Frankie. She wondered if the depot would explode when they did.

"No, it was just the landing gear. I think there was some debris from the last planet stuck in it," said Patav as she flicked through the cameras that surrounded the ship.

And sure enough, a pile of earth accented with tufts of orange grass lay underneath their ship. In view of the camera, a small animal scurried away.

"Welp, this planet is doomed," said Tarke.

"Wait, what?"

"That's a fertisrat. They're an invasive species. Remember, the slimes were talking about it."

"It's just one," said Frankie. "What are the chances it's pregnant?"

100% reported Compi, unrequested.

"Compi's right. Fertisrats are born pregnant."

"OK, well if anyone sees that fertisrat, you're encouraged to kill it," said Frankie, purposely not asking about the biology behind pregnant births.

"We're definitely going to need that bounty now," said Tarke. "Do you know what the fee is for reclamation of a planet that's been taken over by fertisrats?"

Frankie didn't want to know.

"One million credits!" guessed Gail.

"Higher," said Tarke.

On average, two million, eight hundred thousand, and seventy-two credits aided Compi.

"No one asked you... again. But, you're getting warmer."

"Two million, eight hundred thousand, and seventy-three," guessed Gail.

"Gail, the computer wasn't guessing. Tarke's just pulling your chain," reported Lorav.

"Oh," then a moment later, a laugh from Gail.

Meanwhile, Compi's non-guess forced Frankie into capitulation. "Let's go find it before it gives birth. Suit up." And by 'suit up,' she just meant Tarke needed to change out of her oversized t-shirt.

"We're going on an adventure!" she yelled, jumping up. The shirt hiked up to reveal that a shirt was all she was wearing.

"Forg, Tarke."

"What? I gotta breathe. If I can't wear what I want at home... then what is home?" she ended philosophically.

"Your chambers?" asked Patav, but a smile slid onto her face.

"You guys should be happy I call this whole ship home. And I encourage you to do the same... except for you, Gail."

"It's OK, I call the cargo bay my home. If you don't like it, I encourage you to call before you come in," she retorted.

Frankie made a mental note to call and knock from now on.

Suddenly, the ship shook on its tripod and all the lights on the consoles flashed an SOS before going dark.

"OK, that wasn't the landing gear," said Patav.

"What the mevix?!" shouted Frankie toward the space above their head. "We've already skagforgin' landed!"

"Our entire systems array is knocked out. Electronic attack to avoid blowing up this side of the planet with the fuel," said Lorav.

"How long will it take Brian to repair it?" asked Frankie, before she remembered. Then, "Skagforg."

"Yes, skagforg," said Gail, who rarely swore.

It seemed an apt time, though.

FIVE

"Do you think they're going to send ships down here?" asked Patav, shielding her eyes to look up where a spaceship might arrive.

"They disabled our ship, so they know we're not going anywhere," said Frankie.

"And as soon as they see fertisrats on the planet surface, they'll prohibit all aircraft landings per company policy," added Tarke before a surprised, "What is that?"

"Captain said, suit up," Gail defended as she stepped out of the ship wearing a full mech suit. As designed, she towered two feet over everyone. As both a vanity symbol and a marketing ploy, the mech suit had remained enormous to advertise their machinery, despite being largely inefficient and statistically more likely to kill its occupant than to protect him.

"I just meant that Tarke should put on pants," admitted Frankie.

"Isn't it a little redundant to wear a mechanical suit over your bionic features?" asked Lorav.

Indeed, Gail's suit featured a spine-enforced torso and arms decidedly less functional than Gail's artificial muscular hydrostats. The perfunctory arms were outfitted with pincers at their ends and an arthritic range of motion, safety limits necessitated after the Delicatessen Fracturement of 2030.

Gail thought it necessary all the same. "I hate fertisrats, they're a bane to shipping everywhere. You transport one fertisrat and deliver it to a planet and suddenly *you're* the one blacklisted. No, I'm hunting this one down." She shook her head and stared out into the distance.

Frankie followed the determined woman's eyes to the jungle-like terrain surrounding the fuel center. Zimmer 1 was a small planet and Frankie had wondered more than once if they had enhanced the planet with artificial gravity in order to make the place viable. It really wasn't much bigger than Pluto, which had been relegated to un-planetness by Earth scientists, and in the same year, declared by galactic scientists to be the gold standard in planet vs 'other orbiting thing, et al' designation.

Being the yard-stick for planets was actually a promotion over the cold lowliness Pluto experienced, but still the nonscientific community on Earth struggled with

the supposed demotion. The ones who had endured this changeover were called millennials. These millennials had been forced to create inaccurately scaled polystyrene models of their stellar system every year in grade school. Coincidentally, discarded polystyrene had taken over most of their planet. Once space travel became possible for the Earthlings, this ancient generation, who had become insanely rich due to never having bought a place in which to live and destroying basic chain restaurants, paid to have dirt shipped to Pluto to bulk it up.

This, of course, messed with planetary measurements, creating a discrepancy between the designation of planets before and after the Great Millennial Gratification Project. The destruction of multi-universal measurement systems cemented the millennial generation as the generation that had killed everything.

Increasing the gravity of a planet was no easy task. The universe had a delicate balance, and like the arrival of a perpetually pregnant animal species, small things could have a considerable effect. For example, the Great Millennial Gratification Project changed the gravity of Pluto, pulling Earth (which was largely polystyrene at the time) farther from the Sun, solving the planet's global warming problem. While millennials had saved their planet from melting into toxic polystyrene goo, they were still lambasted by one of the few remaining baby

boomers. "Oh now the problem has just disappeared? Huh? Give me back my straws, then," he was reported as saying from his over-sized polystyrene recliner.

While it had worked out well for Earth, changing planetary orbits and gravity fields was not usually met with excellent results. To avoid having a planet collapse on itself and create a black hole (as had happened with Elon Muska II and Elon Muska VII), injection of heavy metals into the bedrock of a planet was always countered with an additional moon, called a stabilitate. A poor name choice as stabilitates often caused rolling earth formations, much like below Earth's Kombucha oceans.

Of course, this is all to say that when Frankie looked out and saw the bright verdant jungle undulating, she wasn't sure if it was the planet's tidal real estate or something extremely large moving through the trees.

The constant break of the earth should have disrupted all life there, but instead, it became a tilling of the soil and trees and plants adapted, by rooting to each other and sitting upon the rolling earth, rather than securing themselves to the earth. It was this adaptation that had led to the changing of the motto, "root yourself," to no longer mean holding your ground, but to remaining upright in the midst of constant change through acceptance, adaptation, and ingenuity. That was a lot to say, so instead they continued to say, "root yourself."

"There it is!" shouted Lorav, pointing up in the trees.

"Mevix, you didn't tell me they climb trees," Frankie swore.

"They don't. He flew up there," replied Tarke.

Frankie gave her a dirty look. "Anything else we should know about this species we're trying to capture? Besides that they can fly and are perpetually pregnant?"

"They do have a natural population density limit. Any guesses?" asked Tarke.

Gail jumped up and down and raised a large mechanical pincer. "Two million, eight hundred thousand, and seventy-two!"

"No. That's not even a density."

"All right fertisrat expert, how many?"

"One fertisrat per fertisrat-space. A fertisrat-space being a measurement specifically created for the measurement of fertisrat density populations. One fertisrat-space is—"

"The size of one fertisrat?" asked Lorav.

"You read my mind, didn't you?" said Tarke, upset she didn't get to finish explaining.

"I finished reading your mind eons ago. It was a cute little story."

"Don't tell me how it ends," rushed Tarke.

"Wait. You're saying they will multiply until they cover the surface of the planet?" asked Frankie.

"Technically they can layer."

"But there wouldn't be enough food."

"They absorb the nutrients of their pregnancies and consume their dead. It's basically a self-sustaining orgy with no need to stop to eat or to pay the electric bill."

No one questioned Tarke's listed reasons. If anyone knew the limits and constraints of an orgy, it would be Tarke.

She read a lot.

"OK, well let's hope it doesn't get to that. Especially seeing as we're possibly stuck on this planet until we study online to become mechanics."

"Is the test multiple choice?" asked Gail, suddenly worried. "Or essay? I suck at essays… and multiple choice."

"The test will be if we can successfully get off this fertisrat-infested planet," replied Frankie.

"Do you think they'll gum up the engine?" asked Lorav.

"Depends on how many fertisrat-spaces an engine is… but uh, yeah, probably. I wouldn't worry; we'll be dead by then," Tarke assured them.

"Why?" asked Frankie nervously.

"Well, our heads are roughly the size of a fertisrat-space. Patav's head maybe two," said Tarke.

That silenced them all for a moment, until—

"Hey, my head's identical to Lorav's! Why are you making fun of me?" asked Patav, who had remained silent even as they discussed fertisrats digging into brains for perpetual orgies.

They all looked at Patav and cocked their heads in different directions and then sort of nodded.

"Your head's bigger, mate," said Lorav.

Patav felt around her head, trying to get a feel for its size. She then approached Lorav and did the same to her head.

"You guys suck," said Patav, not reporting her findings.

Just then, a round brown creature waddled by. It had the loped head of an Earth beaver and a long, hairless, prehensile tail.

"Oh, there's one more thing I need to tell you," said Tarke hurriedly.

"No, I think that's enough," said Frankie, unholstering her plasma shooter and firing on the south-end of the north-bound fertisrat.

A pop and the unmistakable sound of a cheer followed as the fertisrat exploded into colorful confetti twenty fertisrat-spaces away.

"Uh, what was that again?" asked Frankie, suddenly interested again in what Tarke had to say.

"Biologists received endless grants to curb the fertisrat populations, but in the end, they couldn't manage it. So instead they tweaked fertisrat genes to make them fun to kill."

"…but did it cheer?" asked Patav, mortified.

"A modification of their rectums."

"…but, how—" began Gail.

"Gail, please, no," Frankie cut her off. "I killed it. We're in the clear now, right?" asked Frankie. Forty minutes to kill it? Maybe that was a record.

But before Tarke could give another lecture, the head of another fertisrat popped out from the underbrush.

Another small explosion of confetti.

"How many fertisrats are in the average litter?" Frankie was afraid to ask.

"Two million, eight hundred thousand, and seventy-two?" guessed Gail.

"That answer doesn't even make any sense," said Lorav.

"Close," said Tarke.

"How can that be close?" exclaimed Lorav.

"The answer is twenty-two."

"Those numbers are like two million and eight hundred thousand and forty apart."

"Well, they both ended with 'ty-two."

Gail doubled over in laughter, requiring a ridiculous amount of clearance. Tarke, in fact, retreated into the ship.

"Don't you want to leave the suit here?" asked Patav, who didn't fancy getting run over by a laughing Gail.

"Well, the thing is, I'm not wearing any pants."

Frankie shook her head, and pointed Gail in a direction where she could hunt without endangering others. Lorav and Patav went east. Frankie went north. They had twenty-one others to find.

Frankie pressed through the tall monkey grass with her small boots, hoping to cause one to scurry. At the same time, she hoped another didn't fall on her head from a tree.

"That's going to take too long," Tarke called to her. She had exited the ship and now followed Frankie with a large bazooka-type weapon resting on her shoulder. Tarke lowered its muzzle toward the brush beside Frankie.

"I'm not an expert but I don't think blanket weapons fire is going to save this planet."

Tarke ignored her and cocked the weapon. Frankie dove to the side, landing in the prickly brush to avoid being hit. Tarke's lip twitched as she tried to hide her smile. Her weapon blew compressed air like a giant room-temperature hair dryer. It sounded like one too. As dirt

and debris flew, so did the fertisrat. Frankie took aim from the ground, fired, and sprayed herself with confetti. It looked like confetti. It felt like confetti. It smelled like rat innards. Frankie gagged and Tarke could no longer hold her laughter. She fell over, clutching her stomach. Frankie could only hope the smell of the dismembered rodent was a contributing factor to Tarke's convulsions.

They heard a distant cheer. Then another. And another. It appeared the automatic targeting in Gail's mech suit was a force to be reckoned with when it came to opossum-tailed space rats. Gail's comment floated through Frankie's head. *Not this time?*

"I'm forgin' tired of running after these rats," said Frankie, throwing down the air gun she'd operated for the last hour. She wiped the confetti from her brow. Her neck and back ached from bending over or looking into the trees. Why couldn't the stupid things settle in places at eye level?

They had killed thirty-three fertisrats and still no one had the courage to utter what they knew to be true. This was getting out of hand. They had no idea how many were out there, and it was clear that leaving just one would doom the planet.

"Maybe," Patav said, "we should tell someone sooner rather than later. A professional might be able to handle this better."

"Maybe," Tarke said, "we should tell them we saw a fertisrat when we got here."

"We *saw* a fertisrat? No one is going to believe that," said Frankie.

"Have any of you looked closely at the confetti?" asked Gail.

"Um, I try not to. It is rodent guts, after all."

"Yes, but there's writing on it," said Gail. This wasn't the first time Gail had spotted fine print. Her bifocal glasses made everyone wonder if they too needed bifocals.

She peeled a blue speck off the high of Frankie's cheek. Frankie gagged a little. The confetti was challengingly small. Any writing on it would be impossible. Karen pulled out a secondary magnifying glass and attached it to her glasses.

"It says, 'If you are reading this, it has gotten out of hand. Call fertisrat population decimation and damage control.' And on the other side, 'No questions asked' along with a phone number."

"A phone number?" asked Tarke, amazed.

"Yes, an Earth phone by the looks of it."

"Shoot, they should have their own reality TV show."

Gail nodded appreciatively.

"Yeah, then maybe you'd be better at this, Tarke," cut Lorav.

"Hey now, at least I'm trying to help. I'm offering fertisrat fun facts and job leads!"

"Let's call it quits. We're not making any money shooting these blasted things. And all this ruckus is going to drive away the Kieron." Frankie scraped confetti off her leg with the heel of her boot.

"Plus, I need to get out of this suit," remarked Gail. "It's starting to smell a lot like… Gail… in here."

Even covered in rodent organs, everyone made a face.

"Gail, you'll call that phone number… since you're the only one that can see it."

"Are we sure she isn't making it up to go back inside?" asked Tarke.

No one thought there was a chance of that. Still, they instinctively turned to Lorav and Patav for any concern involving intent or deception.

"It has gotten out of hand," they replied, not answering outright.

That was enough for Frankie.

Gail began pulling off outer pieces of the mech suit as soon as she was in sight of the Atalan. The smell of ripe Gail wafted through the air, sending everyone fleeing inside to escape.

RATS & BOLTS

Frankie peeled off her tight suit and dropped it into a biohazard bag, to burn, she imagined. With confetti dotting her face and hands and weaving through her hair, she stepped into the automatic shower. The confetti took on water, elongating. The rainbow colors faded into red tendrils of sinew, fat, and possibly embryos.

All the crew members required lengthy showers, except for Tarke, who knew to scour her skin before showering. Compi reported a backup in the water reclamation system. Mechanic required.

SIX

Frankie was slipping into a fresh suit when Patav's voice crackled through the lines into her room.

Captain? Is everything OK?

"Yes, as far as I know. On my way to the bridge." Frankie zipped up and raced to her intended destination. When Patav got a feeling, Frankie did not dally.

Neither did the women. Lorav and Patav were already there, leaning against their respective consoles.

"What's up?" she asked.

"I didn't notice when we arrived. All I felt was disgust—"

"Yeah, I felt that too," admitted Frankie.

"But now there's this lingering fear."

"Could it just be that one or more of us are afraid we're never getting off this planet and that fertisrats will overtake and eat our unemployed bodies? I mean… hm, that *is* strange."

"No, I mean, maybe. But this fear has a different flavor or sharpness," said Patav, struggling to find the words.

"Is someone else on board?" whispered Frankie.

Patav's eyes lit up. "That's definitely a possibility."

Lorav and Frankie looked around the bridge, as if this knowledge would reveal a stranger in their presence.

"What are the chances…" started Lorav.

"The chances are good," said Frankie. "I mean, unless these are the emotions of a fertisrat?"

Patav shook her head. "It's more nuanced than animal fear, but it's similar. They are scared for their life."

Frankie spun a couple of dials and locked down the ship's escape pods and cargo bay.

Then, over the intercom she announced, "Look, we don't wish you any harm, but we can't have a stowaway on a contracted courier ship. We have to report all occupants. You have five minutes to reveal yourself, else I'll be forced to isolate my crew and vent exhaust back into the ship to flush you out."

A heavy knock landed on the bridge's door. That was fast. No, just Tarke and Gail.

"Why did you give her five minutes? Now we have to wait five minutes." Tarke slipped into her seat, legs propped up. Her mane had been slicked into the shape of the back fin of a particularly sexy personal space ship.

"Spock, I don't know," admitted Frankie. "I just said it. I can't take it back now. It'll seem… unprofessional."

"Unprofessional? Is there proper etiquette for bluffing?"

"I'm not bluffing. I'll fill the place with exhaust."

"And trust that your ship's interior seals are up to code?"

Frankie paused. "Fair point… How much time has passed?"

"I don't know. You're the one that started this arbitrary timer. Did you not check the time?"

"No, I was too busy… bluffing."

"See, now *that's* unprofessional."

Frankie rolled her eyes.

Over the intercom, she announced, "You've got two minutes."

Tarke watched her a moment, then raised her eyebrows at the captain.

Oh, yeah. "Compi, set a timer for two minutes."

"What if you're wrong about two minutes left?"

"What do you mean? She can't argue. I'm the one in control here. If I say there's two minutes left, there's two minutes left."

"Well, if you're in control, why did you give another arbitrary time? Why didn't you just say, 'Reveal yourself now or I'll do this thing'?"

"Shut up."

"I think even if I reveal myself, you can't take off." The strange voice wafting through the speakers made Frankie feel more spooked than victorious in her efforts to communicate with the stowaway. Her voice reverberated, deep and sultry.

"Does that sound evil?" asked Tarke. "She sounds kind of evil."

"Well, she did crash a ship…" reminded Gail.

"Look, we need accurate flight manifests. Come to the bridge and we can discuss your status as a passenger," Frankie tried.

"What if I want to keep things more distant?"

Time's up

"Your time is up. You can —" she looked at Tarke purposefully "— come now or prepare your lungs for carbon monoxide."

"What if I don't have lungs?" Frankie looked to Tarke, who shrugged. "Just kidding. I'm coming. Hold on. I have asthma; don't skagforge me."

There was a lingering knock on the bridge's door.

Frankie's first act as captain had been to turn off the bridge's automatic doors. The bridge was a key part of the ship and to leave it unsecured for convenience's sake was just asking to get hijacked. It was a simple obstacle that wouldn't keep enemies out indefinitely, but would at

least save the crew from getting caught off guard. Considering half the crew jumped at the sound of the knock, the closed door was definitely the way to go. The security monitor showed tendrils floating every way, brushing the door, the camera, the walls. She was definitely their guy.

"Do you have any weapons on you?" asked Frankie through the intercom.

"Just this… air gun? I guess. I couldn't get access to your armory." She held up one of her tendrils to present the object.

"She tried to get into our armory," repeated Lorav as if she was reading her mind.

"At least she's honest," reminded Patav.

Laying down the air gun did little to convince Frankie she hadn't found any more of Tarke's weapons strewn about the ship. The Kieron in slow, bewitching motions, opened her jacket and spun around. Tentillum curled along the hem of the jacket, pulling it up. The girls behind her whistled.

Tarke pointed her weapon at the door as it opened. The woman shuffled in, her tentacles close to her sides as if to restrain them. Her main branches she managed to contain, but their offshoots still moved unceasingly, reaching toward anything nearby. Some occupied themselves by playing with her dark forest green hair,

which wrapped around her shoulders and fell in large swaths that curved at the ends, an imitation of her extremities – which it was difficult, not to mention impolite, to count. The woman was full of shapely protrusions, including full lips and wide hips. One of those hips cocked to the side, creating a surface on which tendrils played.

"Pleasure to meet you, I'm Quaja."

Frankie noticed the nickname and omission of a surname. "I'm Frankie. That's Patav and Lorav. Tarke's the one with the non-air gun pointed at you. And this is Gail." Gail giggled and waved like a shy school girl. Mevix. "We are a courier ship picking up fuel cells."

"Fuel center's closed," she said.

"Yeah, we see that. Like I said, we are couriers and we came to this fuel center," Frankie repeated.

Mevix, she was a bad liar.

Tarke rescued her with an accusation to distract: "We know that fleet up there isn't for us. So it has to be for you."

There was no way she'd be able to explain away an entire corporate fleet.

"They're for me," she admitted. "I stole some fuel from them."

Half-truths. Even though she knew it was a lie, Frankie almost believed her. She was a much better liar.

"That's a big ship, angry over some fuel," said Frankie coolly. "What do you need it for?"

"To barter passage on a ship."

"Then you decided it would just be easier to sneak on board this one?"

"You guys kind of left it open."

"Like unlocked?" Frankie asked, glaring at Gail, who was in charge of the cargo bay doors.

"Like, actually open," said Quaja. Gail's face turned a deep plum red. "Anyway, I'm guessing we both need off this planet. You don't seem to be on great terms with the fleet above us and you've run aground. I'm somewhat of a mechanic. I'll fix your ship, give you the fuel I have on hand, and you'll grant me discreet escape from this planet."

Frankie pretended to think it over, but she could hardly contain her excitement. This bounty hunting thing was easy. They already had her on their ship and now were going to get free mechanical work and fuel to boot.

"Tarke, what's the estimated time on that tow?"

Tarke raised her eyes from some hushed argument she was having with Gail. Then, her eyebrows rose before she caught on. She ran fingers along her tablet. "Current status: three days," she lied.

"Forg it all!" Frankie yelled, making her crew jump. "That is three days we are not making buttloads of courier

money!" An elbow jabbed into her ribs. She quieted. "OK, you fix the ship before the tow arrives, and we will drop you off in the next stellar system. If the tow arrives before you can get us off the ground, then we'll throw you overboard."

"Are we pirates now?" asked a confused Gail.

Quaja's eyelids fluttered. At first Frankie thought Quaja saw through her facade, and maybe she did, but she also appeared grateful. She cleared her throat with a low rumble.

"Well, let's get started," Frankie said before Quaja could respond.

Quaja looked to Tarke then back to Frankie with her unspoken question. Frankie nodded to Tarke, who lowered the weapon's nose, but kept it drawn. Quaja cocked her head from one side to the other as if she found the gesture acceptable.

"May I?" she asked, several tendrils waving toward the engine console. Quaja still didn't trust that Tarke wouldn't shoot her tentacles off.

Quaja wasn't a fool.

With another nod, the Kieron less moved to the console than her appendages pulled her that way. She manipulated the console rapidly, her tendrils moving independently and effectively giving her at least four hands. She ran tests and checked reports that Frankie

didn't even know existed. She could be setting the ship to blow for all Frankie knew.

Frankie looked to Patav and Lorav for some assurance that it would be OK for a wanted saboteur to continue to stand at her ship's console. Patav looked puzzled, but Lorav seemed OK with the thoughts she siphoned from Quaja.

"OK, there's a blockage in the landing gear. It has to be cleaned out from the ground before launch."

"It's probably a bunch of confetti," said Tarke. And with that everyone's stomachs somersaulted. "Gail, you go clear it out."

Gail stopped fluttering her eyes at Quaja to pout. Frankie was unsure if Gail was more disappointed over being assigned rat degunking or having to leave Quaja's presence. The elderly woman had a crush.

"The pulse weapon didn't do any extensive damage, just reset your systems. But, a lot of your systems were already on the fritz. I can do a crude calibration to get you off the ground, but you're riding the edge on a lot of errors. You're going to continue to have issues."

"It's OK. We bypass a lot of them," boasted Lorav.

Quaja blinked at her blankly.

Frankie let out a "What?"

"I mean, not the bad ones."

"The 'bad ones' can't be bypassed," pointed out Patav, who seemed to be familiar with her sister's flight protocols.

Frankie shook her head. "We'll talk about this later." With one more flick of a tendril, Frankie caught sight of their ship manifest in the corner screen, before it was covered by other windows. "I'll escort Quaja to our booster systems. Lorav, Patav, come with us."

Quaja's hands reached out as if to receive her, but then retreated, entwining among themselves. "My apologies," she said out of formality, but circumnutation wasn't really something to apologize for. As an extroverted species, Kieron tendrils always sought interaction with their environment.

As Quaja let her tendrils trace down the paneling of the hall toward the starboard boosters, Frankie hoped the sisters would be able to preempt any wrong turns on several levels. Once at the housing unit for the boosters, Quaja worked deftly, her hands and fingers everywhere. Handing herself tools, holding her own flashlight. Some things she switched out without tools, just wrapping her tactile pads around a bolt and twisting it with ease. She was strong. And she was good. Frankie raised her radiation glasses to watch her work. She wondered how Quaja knew where everything was if she couldn't see it.

Quaja finished in just a few minutes, then asked to go to the next set of boosters. From there she did similar work.

With her arms and part of her head lost inside the ship's machinery, she said, "You know about the bounty, don't you?" It was more a statement than a question.

So, Frankie didn't answer.

Quaja tightened some hidden grimy bolts. "If you're going to sell me out, could I just ask that you hand me over to Vigar Industries? I'm sure they'd be happy to match the bounty of Microlutions."

"Vigar Industries isn't up there to collect the bounty?"

"No, they're out to collect me. As I'm a former employee of Microlutions, they think I have information they can use."

"Do you?"

"Maybe, but I'm sure they know all I've learned. They've been in the business of skagforging Microlutions a lot longer than I have. I just couldn't let that ship reach its destination."

"I heard it crashed near a Pi Zeconis building."

"Yes, the sabotage was delayed. It was never supposed to get that close to its target."

"Wait the target—"

"—was a negotiation talk between Pi Zeconis and several high-ranking officials from Vigar Industries. They

couldn't use weapons without starting an inter-corporate skirmish, so they planned an 'accident'.

"Are you serious?" asked Frankie. She looked to Patav and Lorav, who seemed to believe the story with sad acceptance.

"The commercial wars are no joke. Microlutions has declared potential targets of all competitive infrastructure. The bigwigs just see the numbers. Then with decisions trickling down, suddenly we're driving a fully staffed research ship into a building of employees." Several tendrils coiled into glistening fists, thorny hooks presenting. "So just please, if you have to hand me over – Microlutions is going to execute me as soon as they find me. They don't want me blabbing about their business practices. At least Vigar Industries will torture me for a while before killing me to cover up their business practices. Maybe I can escape. I can't escape dead."

"Are you finished?" asked Frankie.

The woman gave a strange look and realized that Frankie was asking about the boosters.

"Oh yeah, I've been done. I was just trying to plead my case. But, you've got weeks of work that needs to be done when you get back to civilization."

Weeks of work was something Frankie could not afford without weeks of work.

"OK, thank you. We're going to restrain you for our safety and then inspect your work. Then, I guess, we'll figure out what to do with you."

Quaja pulled reluctant tentilla from their small spaces within the depths of the engine, tools in grip.

With Quaja properly tucked in a shipping container, the others returned to the bridge to determine her fate.

Lorav began launch protocol to see if they'd get any errors. They did not; the computer gave the go-ahead. Prudently, Lorav ran a few more tests to see if anything else had been broken or sabotaged during the repairs.

"Well, it works," said Lorav.

"Give me the lowdown, women." Lorav and Patav had listened intently to Quaja's story. Frankie hoped they had gleaned something that she hadn't. "Do you think that Microlutions would kill civilians?"

"I could sense she didn't know if we'd believe that part of that story. That doesn't necessarily mean she's lying though, just that she knows it's a hard-to-believe aspect of her story," said Lorav.

"What about you, Patav?"

"I sensed an urgency for us to believe her. Once again, that could be because they are lies to save her skin or because it's the truth. I will say though, that most people

don't feel that much panic when they're lying. They try to keep composed so they can relay the desired persona."

Really, the sisters weren't that helpful.

"And what's your gut say, Tarke?"

Tarke looked up from her nails, which she was filing into claws.

"Is the question whether we turn her in to Microlutions or Vigar Industries? I vote Vigar Industries. They're right up there. We negotiate a similar payout and we save fuel. Win-win."

It would be easy to mind their own business and do the trade. Let the corporations and Quaja sort it all out on their own.

"What about me?" asked Gail, who had arrived with bionic arms sprinkled with confetti.

"Don't get that skagforg on the bridge. Confetti's like glitter. It gets everywhere," said Tarke. "And we didn't ask you because we know you're crushing on her hard."

"I haven't even said two words to her."

"Exactly," said Frankie, who knew that Gail talked to anyone, anywhere.

The phone rang.

Tarke checked the caller ID. "It's an Earth number."

"Must be the exterminators calling back," said Gail, picking it up.

RATS & BOLTS

"Hello, Franklin and Sons' Courier Services now with Bounty Hunting Services. How may I help you today?"

Frankie had absconded with the title and registration when she left Earth, as it was easier to change the name of a business than to form a new one. Years later and she still hadn't mustered the courage and patience to visit the business licensing planet. It could take an entire revolution of the planet to be seen and told you were in the wrong continental department. Also they probably shouldn't be advertising their bounty services. They were unregistered and, apparently, had a lot of moral distinctions that made it difficult to perform even their first job.

"Uh, yes, this is Fertisrat-B-Gone. We have a service crew coming up on the planet now. They report that there's a large mothership orbiting the planet. Is it yours?"

"Oh my, no, we're on the surface."

"If this is a hunting party, we really have an issue. You see, you can't release fertisrats onto a planet to host a hunting contest or game. They're a very invasive species and we can't just clean up after you. It affects the planets for years to come."

"I thought they said no questions asked," said Frankie quietly. Then overhead she said, "No, we'd never be that reckless. But *that* ship was here before we arrived," trying to throw Vigar Industries under a fertisrat-shaped bus.

"OK. I will be in contact with you shortly."

Gail hung up.

"Gail, please, please, don't tell people we're bounty hunters, because we're not."

RING RING

"Hello, Franklin and Sons' Courier Services now with Bounty Hunting Services. How may I help you today?"

"Yes, this is Vigar Industries." If Frankie's eyes shot pins, Gail would be a pincushion. "You told us you were only here on courier business. And now some exterminators call us and accuse us of some bounty hunting party and using rats to flush out our target."

Fertisrat-B-Gone asked a lot of questions. It was really false advertising. Maybe she'd report them to the Planet of Advertising Affairs and Tolerable Bait-and-Switch.

"Were you the ones that put fertisrats on this planet?" started Tarke. "Because, they're a really invasive species. This isn't fun and games. There are planetary biosystems at stake."

"We're not even on the planet. YOU ARE," yelled the man over the phone.

"Not for long, this place is a mess. We're heading off. Have fun with the exterminators," said Frankie.

"No, if you fly off, we will shoot you down."

"Why? We don't have your tentacle target," replied Tarke.

Frankie wished again to direct metal objects into one of her crew.

"Is that so?"

"Do you think people as inept as those who would release an incredibly invasive species onto a planet would be able to catch a wanted fugitive? Go to Planet Hell."

Planet Hell was actually a lovely tropical planet, but since Earthlings explained how the word was used in their mythology, it had become a rude phrase and a joke, similar to Greenland and Iceland on Earth.

"You will not be going anywhere until we search your ship."

Having done as much damage as she thought possible, Frankie ended the communication.

SEVEN

"OK, I feel we've overstayed our welcome. Let's get out of here," said Frankie, settling into her chair.

Lorav began launch protocols. Patav primed defensive measures in case someone attacked the ship, as they promised to do. Even as the engines fired up, the phone rang.

Frankie told Gail not to pick up. After it rang through to their voice mail, the caller immediately hung up without leaving a message. Then they popped up on their video screen. It was a man at a reception desk. He had on a headset and a name tag. His name tag read 'Tyrese'. Until they told Compi to answer the video call, they would only see and hear him. Not the other way around.

"Hello, this is Tyrese from Fertisrat-B-Gone. We see that you are planning to evacuate the planet. While this is a wise decision, we will still need you to stay in the vicinity while we complete our work. We have more questions for you."

This last statement got the better of Frankie, and she turned on the video call.

"I don't understand. The confetti said that no questions would be asked and now you're saying that many questions will be asked."

"I see the confusion, ma'am. The phone number listed on the graffiti and the promise of no questions were written by the Department of Transplanetary Invasive Minor Species. But because of the enormity of the tasks at hand, they contract out both extermination and investigations of the species known as fertisrats to us."

"So they don't ask questions but pay you to do so?"

"Yes, now you get it. I'm going to have to ask you to stay within orbit if you decide to evacuate the planet."

"And what if we don't?"

"We will send a task force after you."

Great, first Vigar Industries, now Fertisrat-B-Gone.

"And if we find that you are culpable in this ecosystem destruction, we will have to arrest you and press charges. You will find that the Galaxy Court does not look kindly on planetary destruction."

BEEP BEEP

Frankie ignored the indication of a call waiting. "The planet hasn't been destroyed. The rats have only been on the surface for a few hours."

"Currently, you're responsible for the planet call, extermination services, and ecosystem repair. Ecosystem repair may include but is not limited to reformation of planet's crust, transplantation of forests, rehabilitation and reintroduction of incapacitated species, and bariatric surgery for species who gorged on the fertisrat. In some cases, structural damage has occurred and repairs have to be done to the core of the planet. Also if there is any property on the planet, you will be responsible for its replacement, as we have yet to figure out how to get the smell out. I would advise you to refer to both your ship's and your bounty hunter insurance policies. But, historically, the financial burden falls on the individual."

They had maybe one of those insurance policies, maybe. Either way, it would not save Franklin and Sons from going bankrupt.

If it hadn't been time to make their escape before, now it was.

"OK, we will take all of that into consideration. Good luck to your men on the ground."

"Yes, you heard about the team that went offline last week? Possible infestation." Was it called an infestation when the habitat was human? Frankie didn't want to think much more about it. "We will be in touch shortly. Have a great day."

Tyrese hung up and immediately the phone rang again. Frankie groaned.

"Don't answer it," said Frankie.

Shortly another screen popped up. This time it was Vigar Industries.

"We are warning you, do not leave the planet."

"Resistance is futile," joked Tarke.

"I think that's the fertisrats," said Frankie.

"Definitely the fertisrats," said Patav.

As promised, as soon as they started the engine, the ground became speckled with laser sights as Vigar fighter ships took (poor) aim. Rather than immediately launching up, Lorav and Patav tried their luck along the surface, following the rolls of the land surf. Cresting a hill, another wave moved toward them, but this one was more brown than the tropical jungle greens. It took a moment to register that a large sea of fertisrats undulated toward them. Brown fur, pink noses and paws, creepy tails, all flowing in ever-increasing numbers.

"Ugh," said Gail. "Tint the screen 100%." She looked a little green.

"Gail, we can't see now."

"Oh yeah."

"It's fine. They're registering on the radar. Performing evasive maneuvers now." Still, many cheers could be heard. "Deploying anti-laser mirror systems."

Lasers deflected, some rays caught friendly ships, slowing the onslaught.

"Prepare for a subspace jump!"

A few buttons later, Compi announced, *Subspace access unavailable. Please see owner's manual.*

"Mevix," said Frankie. She looked to Tarke. "Go get Quaja."

"Are we going to hand her over to the fertisrats?" she asked hopefully.

"No, we need her to fix the ship."

"You mean the ship she broke?"

"We weren't anywhere near the subspace support. She didn't do this."

"We suck at being bounty hunters," complained Tarke as she exited the bridge. "It looked so much cooler on television."

They were out-engined and out-gunned but these were Lorav's and Patav's, respective and simultaneous, strong suits. They stayed one step ahead, dipping, diving, rolling, not just evading but setting up the ships behind them to cross paths. Finally, four of the Vigar fighters pulled it together and gave chase in a Flying Mallard formation, forcing the Atalan into the path of a bulky ship with bolted paneling. Someone had spray painted PEST CONTROL on the sides.

"Did you try restarting it?" asked Quaja with a polite smile when Frankie buzzed her and Tarke in. Quaja's tendrils flared ever so slightly this way and that to balance against the sub-optimal inertial dampeners, except for one rogue coil which waved aimlessly toward the closest available surface. Quaja reeled in the prodigal but it still gave the appearance of suppressing a festive mood. Could she not take this seriously? They were under attack because of her.

Did they try restarting it? Frankie looked to Tarke, her eyes questioning.

"Of course I did. We might, uh, want to try it again, though," said Tarke lamely.

With a dart of her eyes and an undetermined number of gestures, Quaja asked for permission to move toward the console. Frankie gave a nod. She had nothing else to lose.

"If you've already tried restarting it, let's do a soft reset," she said diplomatically as she pressed a few buttons to turn the subspace widgets offline.

Tarke smiled at the rescue. Frankie could tell she liked her, grudgingly. And if you disregarded the antics of her tendrils, Quaja did seem to be a pleasant person. But, how much of that was her trying to save her skin? Frankie hadn't taken many hostages, but she assumed that politeness and pleasantness was hostage protocol.

Anyone could be nice with a gun to their back. Or could they? Frankie could name a significant number of people who wouldn't be able to do that. People who couldn't find a kind bone in their body even when their lives were at stake. Perhaps she should give Quaja a bit more credit.

"Twenty-seven, twenty-eight, twenty-nine," said Quaja out loud at the end of an initially silent count. She finished by pressing the button to turn the subspace widgets back online. The computer ran through its safety checks and subroutines.

"Compi, subspace widget status?"

Online and functional. Would you like to proceed?

"YES!" they all shouted as Vigar Industries fired a bright red ray towards them.

To the outside observer, the small ship deflected light like a pool of water might, if water could remain in ship shape in outer space. A ripple originated from the subspace turbine and as it spread, the ship disappeared in its wake. The red laser beam shot through the now doughnut hole of the ship. Uninterrupted, the ripple crept to the other edges of the hull, and the ship vanished entirely.

Then, in another instant, a large flash accompanied the reappearance of the same ship four hundred yards to the left.

"WHAT THE MEVIX! We're still here!" shouted Frankie to Lorav.

Lorav swung around in her seat, smashing into Patav, who misfired their pulse weapon.

"Well, excuse me! I thought it would be safer for us to move four hundred yards quickly to avoid that laser. Would you like a more thought-out route with half a ship or would you like to stay in one piece?" She glared at her captain.

Frankie put her hands up in surrender with an "OK, OK," if only to get Lorav to return to her duties.

"Backseat drivers," grumbled Lorav as she turned back around in time to make them disappear and reappear back to the original position before a blue laser beam could strike their ship.

Frankie bit her tongue to avoid pointing out the reason behind the second short jump. Instead, she returned the grumble and shook her head. She looked to Quaja for support, and the Kieron managed a sympathetic smile for her. Frankie was really starting to like her.

Tarke interrupted. "Before we go… are we going to trade her in?"

Frankie didn't even consider it. "These guys have been so rude and bossy. If they'd attack a courier service, they'd

do much worse to their target. I'm not giving them anything."

Patav and Lorav exchanged looks. Tarke argued.

"Thank you," whispered Quaja, her eyes clouding up like swirling galaxies.

"Get us out of here, Lorav," said Frankie.

The ship wrinkled like a blanket in space, then suddenly drew taut before visually collapsing in on itself. The variabilities in deformation could be resolved using the square of the measured length of travel and plotting several relative positions in space, but no one really bothered. In one moment, you were both here and there. If something interrupted destruction or construction on either end, the ship would revert to the other. If both points were deemed obstructed, the ship remained in subspace, a layer of existence throughout typical space and yet separate.

And that's exactly what happened to the Xavier-class courier ship.

As the ship formed on the other side, widgets approximated half the ship would merge into a 3-Texas Asteroid, a near-impossible possibility, when most of space was... spacious. And as the turbine reversed its progress, returning to the space relatively near Zimmer 1 – a laser beam made its way, scraping against the edge of what would have been the ship.

With subspace widgets unable to form the ship within safe parameters at either location, the widgets retracted the ship from both absolute locations and instead chose a relative position within subspace.

"I just want to say," started Patav. "We suck at this bounty hunting thing."

EIGHT

"Compi, windscreen opacity at 40%."

Their windscreen showed the vastness of subspace, which most of their brains interpreted as bright luminescence, throbbing or sparking in clusters.

"It's beautiful. Where are we?" asked Gail.

"Uh, precisely nowhere. This is subspace," said Lorav.

"I've never been to subspace," she whispered in awe.

"Actually we're surrounded by it all the time and passed through the plane often in our travels. The more correct statement would be, you've never been here this long before."

"OK," said Gail, barely listening and instead mesmerized by the sight.

It was a sight Frankie had hoped to never see again, but it was also probably better than the alternatives – getting crushed by a laser weapon or merging into whatever object was on the other side. Using subspace to move around in actual space had become mainstream,

but getting unstuck was still an expensive venture. Frankie couldn't afford their own re-ionizing cannon, nor could she afford not to use subspace. It was a calculated risk Frankie had never calculated. And she'd chalk this one up to variance.

"Any clue where we are?" asked Frankie.

Subspace navigation was virtually impossible. Even now, all the console panel gauges were going berserk.

"I'm running some calculations now," said Lorav, who was busy marking things on her tablet. "Carry the one…" she muttered to herself.

Not one to be dissuaded by transdimensional misplacement, Tarke pressed on. "Does that mean we are delivering her to Microlutions?"

"We couldn't even give her to Vigar," started Patav.

"*Farkhanix* couldn't give her to Vigar," corrected Tarke.

Frankie refused to be distracted by the cheap shot. "I like her."

"I like her too," Gail pied up before devolving into a giggle.

Frankie turned to Quaja. "We're short a mechanic. I'm offering you a probationary position on my crew." Quaja's tendrils flew up in surprise. "—the possibly temporary kind, not the parole kind," she clarified.

Tarke immediately voiced disagreement, but Frankie put up a hand to quiet her. Captain over second. Still, she knew they'd have words, both personal and professional, later. But for now, she was interested in what Quaja had to say.

"Oh wow," Quaja looked surprised and then rather sheepish, "Can I ask what you all... uh, do?"

Everyone exchanged glances. From this vantage point, bounty hunting didn't seem sustainable. And they had been replaced by Instant Teleport!™.

"To be determined," said Lorav.

"And do you all have any funds? Resources besides this ship?"

"Nope!" Gail piped up again.

"Independently owned," said Frankie proudly. "Well, the ship's on lease... OK, so we don't have a lot, but I have a feeling we can help each other out."

"Aren't feelings *her* job?" she asked, a tentacle pressing toward Patav. Then to answer everyone's surprise, she said, "Yes, I know she's an empath. And she's a telepath." And pointing to Frankie, said, "And you have x-ray vision."

Gail's hands went to cover her chest. "What!"

"You didn't think she wore those sunglasses inside just to look cool, did you?" asked Tarke.

"I just thought she was a big fan of Corey Hart," said Gail.

"You've seen too many Earth TV shows," Frankie said. "X-ray vision is not all it's cracked up to be. I'm susceptible to radiation just like you. I could literally fry or mutate myself without these glasses."

"You mean, *these* glasses?" said Tarke, jumping over and ripping them off her face, revealing eyes that Frankie pressed shut. Frankie reached into the chair's side pocket and pulled out another pair, placing them on her face.

Tarke ripped those off too.

Frankie reached and grabbed for a pair in another pocket.

"Mevix, girl," said Tarke, handing over one pair and putting the other onto herself. "You can't see anything through these."

"They've got a lead matrix overlay. It allows minuscule amounts of radiation through in order for me to view the world."

"What does it look like?"

"Like your sight… on a different spectrum."

"So can you or can you not see me naked?" asked Gail, her hands still covering her upper body.

Tarke posed provocatively, her hands to her chest as if she were ripping off her shirt. She leaned forward and then pivoted so her ass could be seen in all its glory.

"I try not to focus on that particular stratum." She turned to Quaja. "It's my hope you permanently join our family as obnoxious as it is, and also that you don't kill us in our sleep or sabotage the ship."

"Actually, about sabotage—" started Quaja.

"I don't want to hear it. Just fix whatever it is you did," said Frankie.

Quaja hurried off the bridge, tentacles flying behind her. Tarke moved to follow but Frankie stopped her.

"We all deserve a chance or two. Don't you think, Tarke?"

Tarke gave a small smile, but still remained arms crossed. She flicked her fingers to the left then the right, the computer picking up her gestures.

An episode of *Cat the Bounty Hunter* popped up on the screen.

"The Fourth Rule in bounty hunting is never to listen to the fugitive. They'll tell you the saddest story and you'll be thinking... maybe I should let him go. But you'll never make money that way. Trust me. They always have a sad story. We all do."

"That we do," said Frankie as she sat down in her captain's chair. "Lorav, you got a place for us to go yet?"

"Aye, captain."

"Then let's go so we can be somewhere again."

*

ABOUT THE AUTHOR

Despite not completing algebra in high school, R.M. Hamrick escaped Georgia Tech with a degree in Biomedical Engineering. She uses this combination of science and doggedness to inject a dose of plausibility into the zombie-filled *Chasing* series. She ignores most of that science in the wacky, all-female cast space opera, *Atalan Adventures*.

Currently partnered with a tantrum-throwing tortoise, she loves board games, craft beer, and odd numbers—the author, not the tortoise. The tortoise loves strawberries, tomatoes, and other red food-stuffs. They both live in Lakeland, Florida which has recently named 'pub subs' as its official currency.

Hamrick chronicles the other side of the page on her Patreon. Join to watch video blogs, read draft snippets, snag advanced copies of ebooks, and autographed paperbacks at Patreon.com/RMHamrick.

MORE BOOKS BY R.M. HAMRICK

ATALAN ADVENTURES

THE CHASING SERIES

ISBN: 978-1-950439-94-2
Zing-O-Matic Publishing paperback edition May 2022
Cover Design by R. M. Hamrick
Editing by Sticks and Stones Editing

ATALAN ADVENTURES

RATS & BOLTS

BOOK ONE

R.M. HAMRICK

ZING-O-MATIC
PUBLISHING